8/13/21
$6.99

CALPURNIA TATE 🐾 GIRL VET

A SQUIRRELLY SITUATION

BY JACQUELINE KELLY

WITH ILLUSTRATIONS BY JENNIFER L. MEYER

GODWINBOOKS   SQUARE FISH

HENRY HOLT AND COMPANY · NEW YORK

SQUARE
FISH

An imprint of Macmillan Publishing Group, LLC
120 Broadway, New York, NY 10271
mackids.com

Our books may be purchased in bulk for promotional, educational, or business use. Please
contact your local bookseller or the Macmillan Corporate and Premium Sales Department
at (800) 221-7945 ext. 5442 or by email at MacmillanSpecialMarkets@macmillan.com.

Library of Congress Control Number: 2018945031

ISBN 978-1-250-21115-6 (paperback)   ISBN 978-1-62779-878-5 (ebook)

Originally published in the United States by Henry Holt and Company
First Square Fish edition,
Book designed by Mike Burroughs
Square Fish logo designed by Filomena Tuosto

1 3 5 7 9 10 8 6 4 2

AR: 4.4 / LEXILE: 700L

For animal lovers everywhere

If my little brother Travis hadn't been so crazy about animals, the War of the Squirrels never would have happened. You're probably wondering what on earth I'm talking about, but if you sit down for a minute, I'll tell you everything, even those parts that are best not talked about. Yep, I'll tell you the whole stinking, underhanded mess. I doubt that anyone else will.

It all started because Travis never met an animal he didn't want to adopt

on sight. The trouble was, many of the animals he wanted to adopt had no interest at all in being adopted. Some of them got quite upset about it. In fact, some of them got downright violent about it, but that didn't always stop him from dragging them home. The only thing that ever really stopped him was the sight of blood or guts or suchlike.

(He had a touchy stomach and was prone to fainting.) Anyway, to understand what happened, we have to look back to springtime, the season when baby animals are born. They're born in spring so that by the time winter comes, they'll be big enough and tough enough to survive the cold and the lack of food. Spring was also the season when Travis was most likely to bring some kind of animal—any kind of animal—home.

We had a few barn cats who had kittens in the straw every spring, to Travis's delight, and they kept him busy

4

for a while. Then there was Idabelle the Inside Cat. She was the only one allowed inside; she lived in the kitchen and kept down the mice. Idabelle was also the only cat who'd never had kittens. That spring she grew fat from her steady diet of mice. At least that's what we all thought.

Then one night she started pacing and yowling and, to our surprise, crawled behind the stove and gave birth not to a litter of kittens but to one very large kitten. Nobody had ever seen a kitten like this before. He was easily the size of two regular kittens.

We called him Thud because he was such a bruiser. (I know you think this story is about squirrels, and it is. Trust me, I'm getting there.)

Our cook, Viola, who loved Idabelle, also doted on Thud. Travis did too, naturally. The only one not thrilled about him was Mother, who hadn't counted on two cats living in the house. She had a hatred of fleas but was willing to put up with the baby for a while. There was no resisting Thud, he was that adorable. Idabelle happily nursed him in her basket by the stove, although they were soon overflowing the sides.

"Humph," said Viola. "Looks like we need a bigger basket."

She found an old laundry basket, lined it with a towel, and moved Idabelle and Thud into it. And that should have been all there was to tell.

But no. The story was really just beginning.

Viola and I were enjoying a glass of lemonade in the kitchen, admiring Idabelle and Thud, when Travis burst in from the back porch. He was holding to his chest a small bundle wrapped in a bandanna. Uh-oh. I knew what that meant. So did Viola.

She eyed him suspiciously. "What you got there? It better not be no live thing."

Travis turned his best sunny smile on her, saying, "Don't worry, it won't take up much room. And we don't even have to feed it. Idabelle will. I hope."

He pulled back the flap of cloth. There on his palm lay a newborn squirrel, tiny, helpless, and cute as can be. (It turns out that baby squirrels can give kittens a real run for the money in the cuteness race.)

"Aww," I said. I couldn't help myself. Even the flinty Viola softened when she saw it. "Where'd you find it?" I asked.

"It was on the ground, I swear."

I squinted at him. "You didn't pull it out of the nest?"

"Never. I wouldn't do something like that."

Well, that was a big fat lie if ever I'd heard one. "Ha! I know you, Travis Tate, and that's exactly the kind of thing you'd do. Don't deny it."

"That's true," said Viola, nodding. "The boy would do that."

Travis flushed. "Well, okay, maybe I've done that once or twice before, but not this time, I swear!"

The squirrel coughed feebly.

"It was lying flat on the ground. It was going to die if I just left it there."

The poor thing struggled to lift its head and fell back on my brother's palm, exhausted from the effort. I'd seen many pitiful things in my life, but this was pretty near the top of the list.

"Are you going to get up and feed it during the night?" I said. "Something that size probably needs to eat every hour or so."

Travis smiled.

"And don't look at me," I said, "because I'm not doing it."

His smile grew bigger. "I thought Idabelle would do it."

We all turned and looked at Idabelle nursing Thud in the basket. They were both purring loudly. Thud pawed at his mother's fur, "making muffins," as we called it.

I looked at the squirrel and said, "You're going to . . ."

"I think it'll work, don't you?"

13

Viola muttered, "Sure, if she don't eat it first."

Travis took the tiny, limp figure and placed it up against Idabelle's warm furry belly next to Thud. She looked at it in what I can only describe as surprise. Then she carefully sniffed it from head to tail. We all held our breath while she decided whether the newcomer was dinner or not. Then she started licking the baby vigorously, and we all sighed in relief. The squirrel started to nurse, and from that moment on, Idabelle treated it exactly the way she treated Thud. As family.

"I've been thinking about what we should call him," Travis said. "How about Fluffy?"

"What?" I said. "That doesn't suit him at all."

"Sure it does. He's going to have a nice fluffy tail when he grows up."

"Fluffy is a cat's name," I said.

"Well, look, Callie," he said, gesturing at the basket, "Idabelle already thinks he's a cat, so that makes him sort of a cat. An honorary cat. Which means we can call him Fluffy."

So Fluffy it was.

3

Mother swept through the kitchen, her long skirt swishing. She glanced once at Idabelle and walked briskly out to the back porch. Where she stopped, turned, came back inside, and pointed at the basket. She spoke very slowly: "What. Is. That. Thing."

I looked around for Travis, who was, naturally, nowhere to be seen. Sometimes he would cling to you worse than a sticker burr, but when you really needed him, he was gone.

I said, "Well, um, I really think you should ask Travis about that, uh, 'thing.'"

"Travis is not here. Therefore, I cannot ask him about it. Yet you, Calpurnia, stand right before me. And that is why I am asking you." She tapped her foot the way she did when her patience was running out. The more irritated she grew, the faster she tapped.

I knew that signal well,
probably better than
any of her other
children.

"When were
you going to
tell me? Or
were you
all just
hoping I
wouldn't
notice
it?"

"Uh, that's Fluffy. It's a . . . well, it's a baby squirrel."

"Yes, I can see that." Her foot tapped faster.

"Travis found it on the ground. He brought it home hoping that Idabelle would take to it, and look!" I gestured toward the basket like a magician pulling a rabbit out of a hat. Fluffy and Idabelle and Thud lay tangled together in a ball of complete, furry happiness. "It worked! Isn't motherhood grand?"

Mother narrowed her eyes at me, and I could tell she wasn't finding motherhood so grand at this very minute. "This will never do. Fetch Travis right away. We can't raise a wild animal in the kitchen."

I found Travis in his room and told him what had happened. "We can't just throw Fluffy out," he said. "He'd die out there on his own. And Idabelle's heart would be broken."

"Then you better go downstairs and convince Mother. She's really peeved this time."

Travis had a long history of bringing home wild animals, but in the past he'd usually hide them away in the barn. Let's see, there'd been a couple of skunks, an owl, a porcupine, countless cats and dogs and rabbits, you name it. Sometimes he got away with it, and sometimes he didn't. Clearly this was one of those "didn't" times.

I followed him downstairs and hid in the hallway while he went into the parlor to argue his case.

"I have noticed," said Mother in a frosty tone, "that there seems to be a wild animal living in our kitchen."

"Well, Mother," said Travis slowly, "he's not exactly what you'd call 'wild.' He's already pretty tame, if you ask me. He lets me pet him and everything."

"That's not what I mean, and you know it."

"Yes, Mother, sorry. His name is Fluffy, and I found him on the ground. You can see he's just a *baby*. If we keep him a little longer, he'll have a fighting chance. And he doesn't cost anything. And he's no trouble, really. Callie and I don't even have to get up in the night to feed him."

What? Wait. Why was he dragging my name into this? For once, I was entirely blameless. I almost shouted, "Fluffy is not my fault!" But then I figured it was better to keep my mouth shut and not draw attention to myself. Mother disapproved of eavesdropping, although I don't know why. I myself have always found it to be a perfectly good way of gathering information.

There was a pause while Fluffy's fate hung in the balance. Then Travis pulled out his secret weapon: He started pleading with her. When the boy put his heart and soul into defending an animal, few could resist him. His soft heart and sunny smile were real forces to be reckoned with. My brother loved all animals and was convinced that the rest of the world did—or should—too.

I almost felt sorry for Mother. She sighed, and I knew he'd won her over. At least for a while.

"Ah," said Granddaddy, looking at Fluffy, "I see we have a house-guest from the family Sciuridae. The name comes from the Latin word *sciuris*, meaning a tail that throws a shadow. It is a type of rodent, which means its front teeth will grow several inches per year and will keep growing its whole life. You'll need to give it a small piece of wood to gnaw on to keep the teeth from getting too long. One of my men had a pet squirrel during the War. It perched on his shoulder and chewed bits of bark while we marched, and slept in a pocket he had sewn inside his shirt. He called it Johnny Reb."

"Really? I'd been thinking Fluffy was the only one."

"They are not uncommon as pets, just as long as you get them at a very young age, like this one here."

We stared down at Fluffy. He looked right at home.

"What happened to Johnny Reb?"

"One sunrise we came under surprise attack by the Yankees. It got frightened by gunfire and ran to the top of a very tall tree. There was no time to coax it down. We had to retreat and leave it behind."

"You mean it was just . . . gone?"

"I regret that we never saw it again. It was quite a charming little animal."

I thought of Johnny Reb's owner. But then, could you really own a wild creature? Maybe *owner* wasn't the right word. Maybe *friend* was the right word. He must have been brokenhearted. So many hearts were broken in the War.

"Well," Granddaddy said after a moment, "shall we be off?"

"Yessir." We went out the back door and decided to head upriver for a change. As we walked along the deer path next to the river, Granddaddy talked about the order Rodentia. This includes rats and mice, chipmunks, guinea pigs, woodchucks, beavers, and porcupine. They all spend their whole lives gnawing away.

He told me how rats had been unfairly blamed for spreading the Black Plague around the world hundreds of years ago and that it was actually the *germs in the fleas on the rats* that spread it. But, of course, this was long before there were microscopes and long before anybody knew about germs. People could only see the rats, and since the plague seemed to go where the rats went, they had to be causing it. Right?

But not so. This was another case of what Granddaddy called "jumping to the wrong conclusion based on faulty information." He said that there was a lot of that about. You had to be smart, and careful, to guard against it.

"Keep in mind, Calpurnia, that there is no point in gathering information unless you are certain it is *correct* information."

"Yessir." I pulled my Scientific Notebook and a stub of pencil out of my pinafore pocket and wrote this down.

We passed several adult squirrels on the way, chattering and scolding us

from the
safety of
the trees.
I wondered
if one of them
might be
Fluffy's mother.
How on earth
could you tell?
They all look alike,
at least to the human
eye. But then, maybe we
humans all look alike
to squirrels. Hmm, an
interesting thought, that maybe

a squirrel couldn't tell the difference between me and my grandfather with his long white beard.

We sat for a while, ate our sandwiches, and wandered on. We were about a mile from home when we heard it: a heavy crashing sound up ahead.

Granddaddy stopped in his tracks. He turned to me and said in a low voice: "Get off the path. Hide behind a tree. Now."

I had no idea what he was talking about, but I could tell from the urgency in his voice that it was important. I quickly did as he told me, and we stepped behind the nearest oak, which wasn't quite large enough to completely hide us both. I was about to ask him what was going on when he signaled with his finger to his lips to stay quiet. The crashing noise grew louder. Was it a bobcat? No, no, a bobcat would not be any threat to us; we wouldn't have to hide. And this thing—whatever it was— was making too much noise to be a bobcat. Was it a black bear? It was loud enough, and there were still a few of them around. In that case, we might be in real trouble. I cast about for a weapon of some sort. I myself had nothing except a notebook and a dull pencil. I wanted to ask Granddaddy if he had a knife in his satchel, but he'd told me to be quiet.

It was coming closer. Now we could hear an ugly grunting and squealing.

Out of the bush burst a hairy, black monster, running at full speed along the path. It was about the size of a half-grown bull, but it was not a bull. It was a hideous beast I'd heard of but never seen. A wild pig. A feral hog. Big enough to throw a man to the ground, with fierce curling tusks sharp enough to slash him open. Strong, smart, and fast. Oh, and famous for its bad temper.

I looked sideways at Granddaddy with wide eyes. Were we going to have to climb the tree? Were we going to have to fight it with rocks and sticks? He motioned me to be still.

The hog slowed to a trot and turned to look in our direction with mean, little piggy eyes. It sniffed the air with its bristly snout. It seemed to be making up its mind about something. Then out of the brush ran four smaller pigs, her offspring. *Oh no!* The most dangerous of animals, a mother with her

babies. She'd fight to the death to save them from harm. She grunted at us from deep in her chest. Could she see us? If she was like an ordinary pig, her sense of smell was much stronger than her eyesight. She snuffled and sniffed.

Every instinct in me screamed that I should run or hide or pick up a rock or do *something*. But Granddaddy stood as still as a statue. So I did the hardest thing I'd ever done in my life: I stood like a statue beside him.

I told myself, *Don't move, Calpurnia. Don't you run. Don't you climb. Don't you move, don't you dare.*

It felt like an eternity, but it must have been only a couple of seconds before we heard the most wonderful sound in the world: the baying and yelping of our neighbor's hound dog, Matilda, coming down the trail.

The mother hog screamed in rage and took off, her babies right behind her. A moment later they were gone from sight. You'd never have known they'd even been there.

Granddaddy and I stepped out from our hiding place.

"That—that was a close one," I stammered.

"It was indeed," said Granddaddy.

My legs were trembling and I wished they'd stop. Granddaddy didn't look ruffled at all. (I guess when you've fought the Comanche and Yankees both, there isn't much left that can shake you.)

But the excitement wasn't over yet, because right then Matilda came crashing down the trail, barking and slobbering, her long ears flapping. We were mighty glad to see her, but she was too excited to stop and give us her usual friendly greeting. I jumped at her and tried to grab her collar, but she was

moving so fast that she got clean away
from me and kept on running.

"I sure hope she doesn't catch up to
them," I said in a shaky voice. "Or if

she does, I hope she's smart enough to keep out of range." A mother hog that size could tear apart a lone dog. It would take a whole pack of dogs to bring her down.

"I certainly hope so. Let us head back. I think that's enough excitement for one day." He held out his hand, and I took it. His hand was so big, it completely enclosed mine. My legs slowly stopped trembling. We walked all the way home like that.

That night my father announced at dinner that one of the neighbor's dogs had chased a feral hog.

"Oh!" I said without thinking. "That must—"

Granddaddy cleared his throat. He shook his head the tiniest bit in warning, and I clamped my mouth shut.

"Yes?" said Mother. "'That must' what?"

I suddenly realized that if my parents had known we'd been in danger from the hog, they'd never let me go exploring with Granddaddy ever again. Heck, they'd never let me out of my room ever again. What an idiot I was!

"Oh, nothing," I muttered. "I was thinking of, uh, something else."

This earned me a round of funny looks from everyone at the table except Granddaddy, who calmly chewed his way through his steak. Then Father went on to explain that the hog had ripped the dog's ear open. The neighbor was unhappy because not only had all that ham and bacon gotten away, he'd had to pay Dr. Pritzker—the animal doctor—to sew the ear back together.

Too bad. I'd watched the doctor sew a ripped ear before. I would have done it for free, just to get the practice.

T hud and Fluffy grew quickly. As soon as they were big enough to get out of the basket, they took to tumbling and crawling and batting at each other all across the kitchen floor. I would have thought Viola would have had a fit at the thought of a squirrel in her domain, but her love of Idabelle and Thud was so great that it spilled over onto Fluffy as a form of, well, if not exactly love, at least some tolerance.

Soon Fluffy was big enough to eat solid food. We gave him tiny bits of dried apple and slices of carrot, which he loved. And, of course, he was nuts about nuts. (Ha!) I gave him one of Mother's empty spools of thread to gnaw on. It was just the right size. He clutched it in his paws and chewed on it every day. His fur was as soft as Thud's. If you stroked him gently, his eyes would droop shut with pleasure. After a few minutes he would fall asleep, just like a regular kitten.

Then the trouble began. As soon as he was strong enough, he started climbing. He'd climb anything, including people. He'd scamper up your legs and arms, leaving a trail of tiny, painful scratches the whole way. This was charming only the first couple of times. He liked to climb as high up in the kitchen as he could get, which I guess is only natural for a tree dweller. He climbed on top of the cabinets, taking in everything below with his shiny black eyes.

Viola was cooking one afternoon when I walked into the kitchen in search of a glass of lemonade. Fluffy and Thud were tumbling over each other in the corner in a mock battle. I must have startled Fluffy because he suddenly broke it off and sprang onto one of the roller blinds. It rolled up with a loud *snap*, taking Fluffy up to the ceiling with it. Now it was Viola's turn to be startled. She screamed approximately like this: "EEEEEEE!"

This in turn startled me, and I jumped about a mile. And then it was Mother's turn to be startled, and she came running in from the parlor.

"What's wrong?" she cried, no doubt expecting murder and mayhem from the sound of things. She then startled Fluffy, who leaped onto the clock on the wall. The only calm one left in the room was Idabelle, who lazily cocked one eye open to check on her children, then rolled over in her basket and went back to sleep.

Viola shook her wooden spoon at Fluffy, saying, "You want to end up as squirrel stew? 'Cos I can make that happen, mister."

Fluffy sat on top of the kitchen clock and chittered. Mother looked as if she was getting a headache and wisely backed out of the kitchen.

But Fluffy had discovered a quick and fun and easy way to reach the ceiling via the blinds, and he regularly jumped on them and rode them up. Viola, always busy at the stove, never got completely used to it. She still jumped and threatened him every time, but her screaming got quieter, so there was that.

Whenever Idabelle and Thud went outside, Fluffy tagged along behind them in the grass. But the first tree they came to, he would shoot up, leaping from branch to branch to keep up with his mother and brother below. Sometimes he scampered along the clothesline off the back porch. You had to admire his acrobatic performance, at least until he stopped to gnaw on the wooden clothespins, and then we had to divert his attention to some other project before Viola or Mother caught him at it.

We finally had to accept that Fluffy was now very unhappy living at floor level. His days in the basket were over, no matter how much we threatened or encouraged him to stay there.

"We have to figure something out, Travis, before Viola kills him. And us. And I'm tired of all these scratches all over me." I showed him my arms. I looked like I'd been dragged sideways through a prickle bush.

Fluffy looked up as if he knew we were talking about him. His cheeks were overstuffed with pecans, and he looked like he had a bad case of the mumps.

"But Callie," Travis said, "look at how cute he is."

"I know he's cute, but we have to make him cute somewhere else so he doesn't drive everybody crazy. He's got to quit riding the blinds."

"So," Travis said, "what if we build him a home up high? And a way to get there?"

Sometimes my little brother surprised me. "What do you have in mind?" I asked. "Some kind of basket? How about a birdhouse?"

"I was thinking of some kind of hammock."

"Really? Made out of what?"

"I don't know," he said. "But let's go out to the barn, there's sure to be something there."

We scrambled around
in the barn, looking at
bits of this and
scraps of that,
until finally we
came up with
just the right
thing: an old
piece of canvas

that we turned into a tiny hammock. We tacked it up high in the far kitchen corner. He also added a length of slender rope hanging down to act as Fluffy's own private staircase. Fluffy stopped riding the blinds and scampered up and down the rope instead. He seemed very happy up there, well out of Viola's way.

The only trouble was Thud got it into his head one day to follow his brother up to this perch above the cabinets. He made it about halfway before falling back to earth, almost ending up in the soup pot. (And in case you're wondering, yes, he did make a really loud *thud* when he landed.) Cats may be good climbers, but squirrels are *really* good climbers. Viola shrieked at that, too. There was quite a bit of shrieking in the kitchen that summer.

Then one unfortunate day it was Fluffy's turn to shriek. Travis went out the back door but didn't realize Fluffy was following him. The screen door slammed shut on Fluffy's tail. Fluffy screamed like a screech owl, and I came running. The end of his tail was sticking out sideways at a sickening angle.

"Oh no!" Travis cried, and scooped him up. Fluffy cried out *chip-chip-chip* in distress. "Callie, help me, what do we do?"

I expected Travis to keel over into a faint at any second. (He was prone to that sort of thing whenever an animal was injured.) But there was no visible blood, so he managed to stay upright.

"Put him in his basket and keep him there. I'll get the first aid kit."

I ran off to the bathroom, where we kept a tin box of bandages and ointments. Living on a farm with lots of animals and machinery, folks were always getting cuts and scrapes that weren't bad enough to call Dr. Barker, the

people doctor. We often had to doctor ourselves.

I ran back with the box. Travis was petting Fluffy to keep him calm.

He asked, "Should we take him to the vet, do you think?"

Dr. Pritzker's job was to look after cows and horses and valuable farm animals. Sometimes he'd let me follow along after him, and I'd learned a few things along the way.

"I think I can fix him," I blurted. Then I thought about it some more. "Probably."

"Really? You can do that?"

"Well . . . maybe." I knelt down and looked at Fluffy's tail. The good news was that the rest of him looked all right. The bad news was that I was going to have to straighten out the kink. Dr. Pritzker had taught me that with a broken bone it was important to try and put it back where it was supposed to be. In other words, return it to its original position as much as possible. Once you'd done that, you had to hold the bone in place with a splint until it healed.

Did squirrels have bones in their tails? I didn't know. But I knew that

Idabelle had lots of little bones in her long tail. I'd felt them. She needed her tail for balance, so I figured Fluffy probably did, too.

"Here comes the hard part," I said.

"Uh, what?"

"I'm going to pull on his tail to straighten it out. He won't like it one bit. You'll have to hold him still."

"Oh no. Isn't there another way?"

"Not unless you want him to spend the rest of his life like that. I mean, he looks pretty strange, but that doesn't really matter so much. The important thing is that I think his balance will be bad. He might not be able to climb anymore, and that's no good if you're a squirrel."

"I guess not." Travis looked downcast. "Do I have to watch? Maybe we could get someone else to hold him."

"He's your pet, you need to hold him. But you don't have to watch."

"Okay." Travis petted Fluffy, who by now had quieted down.

I ripped some rolls of gauze into narrow strips for our tiny patient. "All right, hold him tight now. He's not going to be happy."

Travis muttered, "Me neither." He

adjusted his hold and turned his head away.

I thought, *All right, Calpurnia, if you're going to do it, do it fast. It'll be easier on all of us. Pull fast and straight. Go on, fast and straight.*

I gently took hold of the end of Fluffy's tail. Before he could figure out what was going on, I yanked it. I felt and heard a very faint *click* under my hand as the bone slipped into place. "EEEEEEE!" Fluffy screamed, reminding me a whole lot of Viola. Out of all the many screams I'd heard in the kitchen, this one was the grand prize winner. He thrashed and scratched at

Travis, who yelped and let him go.
Fluffy ran up the cabinets to the safety
of his hammock. His tail looked
straight—or at least straighter—as
best I could tell. He scolded us at ear-
splitting volume.

Viola came running from the pantry. Mother came running from the parlor.

"I think you did it, Callie!" yelled Travis over the noise.

"Did *what*?" cried Mother. We could barely hear her. "What happened? Who's hurt?" She stared at us wildly, confused that both her children were upright and neither one was bleeding.

Travis yelled, "Fluffy got hurt, and Callie fixed him."

"Then why is it making so much noise? What's wrong with it? For pity's sake, make it stop!" She put her hands over her ears. "I can't hear myself think."

"It's just that the fixing part hurt," said Travis, "and he's not happy. I know what he needs." He went into the pantry for a couple of shelled pecans and then dragged out the stepladder. Fluffy watched all this and got slightly quieter. Travis climbed up the ladder to the hammock and held out a nut. Fluffy grumbled a little longer, then reached for the nut and stuffed it into his cheeks, and the terrible noise suddenly stopped. The kitchen fell silent. Except for the faint crunching of a nut.

I needed to splint the tail to keep it still, but I couldn't get near him. Fluffy figured his friends had attacked him for no good reason, and he kept a wary distance. The tail seemed to heal up fine over the next few weeks without splinting. But it took a whole lot of time and a whole lot of nuts for him to forgive me.

I t was the fall, and the beginning of
hunting season for Father and Ajax,
his prize bird dog. Ajax had finally
recovered from getting quilled by a
porcupine. Twice. That is to say, he had
recovered from his physical wounds.
But every time he went out hunting, he

spent much of his time looking around scared, as if expecting a porcupine to leap out from behind a bush at any moment. (I guess you'd act the same way too after getting a face full of quills—twice.)

Anyway, autumn was getting on, and
it was time for the Fentress Fall Fair.
Every year young people competed for
prizes for the best livestock and
handicrafts and baked
goods. There were
prizes for cows
and sheep and

goats and rabbits; there were prizes for pies and preserves and knitting and tatting. There were prizes for all sorts of things. And this year there was a hunting prize for boys aged ten to fifteen.

Hunting what? you may ask.

Answer: Why, hunting squirrels.

You may wonder why. Part of it was that the squirrel population had taken a sudden jump this year, and they were chewing up the local pecan growers' nuts at an amazing rate. The growers had banded together and come up with the idea of a squirrel shoot to help save their crops and improve their profits.

Part of this was a way for boys to get started in the hunting life without having to face down something big enough to fight back, like, say, a feral hog. Actually there were two prizes up for grabs: one for the most squirrels killed in one day and another for the biggest squirrel overall.

Travis was deeply offended by this, partly on his own account and partly on Fluffy's behalf. "Why do they have to kill squirrels?" he said. "Squirrels never hurt anyone."

Now, this was perfectly true. I mean, what else could they do besides drop nuts on your head? *Chatter* you to death? On the other hand, there were some families at the far end of town that would go hungry if they didn't have a squirrel for the pot. (Travis knew this, but I didn't see any point in reminding him.) Now he had the perfect excuse to keep Fluffy inside at all times, safe from the line of fire.

There was a mean boy at school, Woodrow Chadwick, who bragged about what a great shot he was to anybody who would listen.

"I'm going to win those prizes—*both* of them—so the rest of you might as well just stay home. Don't even bother to show up."

I didn't like Woodrow one bit, and he didn't like me either. But he and my older brother Lamar were friends, so I had to put up with him coming by our house every now and then. Even so, when he visited, he kept his distance from me. You see, I might have . . .

possibly, maybe, mostly accidentally, kind of on purpose, sort of . . . slugged him. And even if I *had* done that, it was only because he'd insulted Granddaddy. How could anyone stand for it? This was not permitted.

Anyway, Woodrow told Lamar he was spending hours practicing with his uncle's .22 rifle, shooting at old tin cans. I paid him no mind.

Finally the big day came. A dozen or so boys headed out into the woods at sunrise with their pellet guns and rifles. The rules were that you had to shoot as many squirrels as you could before noon, then bring them in for judging at the cotton gin. The three judges were the postmaster, the grocer, and Dr. Pritzker.

At high noon, a small crowd watched as the boys came trailing back along Main Street. Some of them hadn't bagged a single squirrel and looked pretty sheepish. One boy had three, another had five, and Woodrow had six. Ugh. He'd won, just as he'd predicted. It was hard to see a braggart turn out to be right about, well, anything.

So that part of the contest was over. That part was no problem. The problem was the next part.

The grocer had brought his scale, and the judges started weighing the squirrels. Most of them were in the range of two pounds or so. They were just getting to Woodrow when up trotted Travis, holding a cardboard box.

Uh-oh.

He walked up to the judges and said politely, "I'd like to enter my squirrel in the biggest squirrel category." He held out the box, which chattered unhappily.

"What have you got in there, son?" said the grocer.

"It's my squirrel, Fluffy."

"Sounds like you got a live one in there," said the postmaster.

"Yessir. And he's a pretty big one, too."

Woodrow sneered and said, "You can't enter a live squirrel."

"Why not?" asked Travis.

Woodrow and the judges looked taken aback.

The grocer said, "Well, I, uh . . . I don't think the contest is for live ones."

"I read the rules," said Travis. "They don't say anything about it having to be a dead squirrel. Wouldn't you rather have a live one, anyway? They're much nicer, don't you think?"

Fluffy squeaked and scratched at the box, clearly agreeing that live squirrels were indeed much nicer than dead ones.

Dr. Pritzker pulled a piece of paper from his pocket and looked it over. He laughed and said, "The boy's right, you know. It says right here, 'prize for the largest squirrel entered.' It doesn't say largest *dead* squirrel entered." He grinned at Travis. "I say we let him enter."

The other two judges hesitated but then nodded in agreement. Woodrow pouted and glared at Travis.

Good. Anything that made Woodrow pout and glare was fine with me.

The grocer asked, "How are you going to weigh it, son? We can't include the weight of the box; that wouldn't be fair."

"Don't worry," said Travis, opening the box, "he's tame, and I put a string around his neck." He reached in and pulled out Fluffy, petting him to calm him before setting him on the scale. Fluffy looked around, alert but not panicky. He was pretty used to people by then. And Travis was right: A live squirrel was so much nicer than a dead one.

"Goodness, that is one big specimen. What did you raise it on?"

"I really didn't do all that much," he said modestly. "It was mostly our cat Idabelle who raised him."

"Your cat, you say? This here squirrel was raised on cat's milk?"

"That's right."

"Well, I'll be danged."

Fluffy sat on the scale, looking right at home and very cute. You'd have thought he'd been trained for this moment.

The postmaster read the numbers and announced, "Three pounds, eight ounces," while the other judges leaned in to confirm.

"Right," said Dr. Pritzker, making a note of it.

Travis petted Fluffy, gave him a slice of carrot, told him he was a good boy, and put him back in the box.

Then it was time to weigh Woodrow's squirrels. One was clearly a lot bigger than the others and might even give Fluffy a run for his money. But Woodrow wanted to weigh the smaller ones first, making a fuss about putting them on the scale himself. They all weighed quite a bit less than Fluffy.

Then Woodrow picked up the biggest one and put it on the scale so gently you'd have thought it was breakable. It had to be a pretty old squirrel, because it was kind of lumpy and misshapen. Or maybe there was something wrong with it.

The judges leaned in. I noticed that Woodrow looked nervous.

"Four pounds even," said the postmaster. "Looks like we have a winner."

We all applauded politely, even me, trying to be a good sport. Travis looked a little downcast, so I said, "Don't worry about it. Fluffy is much nicer than that old thing. Why, just look at it; it must have some kind of disease."

I noticed that Dr. Pritzker was giving it a funny look as well. I sidled over to him and whispered, "Is there something wrong with it, Dr. Pritzker? Why does it look like that?"

"Hmm," he said, and reached out to lift the squirrel from the scale.

"I'll get it!" cried Woodrow, lunging forward.

But it was too late. Dr. Pritzker was lifting it by the tail.

And then it happened. A whole stream of little metal pellets fell out of its mouth, making a merry *plink-plink-plink* on the pan of the scale.

Everybody froze. It took us all a moment to understand that the squirrel had been stuffed with BBs. To make it heavier.

We all looked at Woodrow, who turned white as a sheet in front of our eyes. I didn't know it was possible for a living human boy to be that color.

"I—I," he stammered. The blood rushed back to his face, now the color of a boiled beet. "I—I—don't—don't know how that happened." He looked like he was going to be sick.

We all stared at him. Nobody said a word. He turned and bolted in the direction of his home. Travis stood there looking shocked.

"Hey, Woodrow!" I shouted. "You forgot your lousy, old squirrel." (Yes, I know it wasn't the nicest thing in the world, but I was furious. He'd tried to cheat my little brother.)

Some other folks in the crowd cried "Cheater!" and "Boo!" after him.

Dr. Pritzker shook the corpse, and a few more pellets dropped out. Now the squirrel looked a whole lot smaller and not so lumpy. Dr. Pritzker swept the

pellets into the grass and dropped the
body back on the scale in disgust. We
could all see that it really weighed only
two pounds.

The judges gathered in a huddle. I
could tell that none of them were in the

mood to give Woodrow any kind of prize for anything. After a minute, Dr. Pritzker turned to the crowd and said, "It is the judges' decision that Woodrow Chadwick deserves no prize at all and is disqualified from the entire competition. Where's the boy who bagged five squirrels? Come on up here, son. We're giving you the prize for most squirrels shot."

The boy looked stunned but happy to accept the prize of a handsome folding pocketknife with a horn handle. Everyone clapped for him.

"Next," said Dr. Pritzker, "the prize

for the biggest squirrel goes to Travis Tate."

"And Fluffy!" Travis called out.

"Right. And, uh, Fluffy. Come on up here."

The postmaster presented the prize to Travis, another pocketknife. "It's just the right size for skinning squirrels," he said, only half joking.

Ugh. Travis looked offended and nearly handed it back. "Don't worry," I said. "You can use it for all sorts of other things. You can sharpen my pencils so I can make my Scientific Observations in my notebook. My pencils need sharpening every day. And you can use it to cut bark for Fluffy. After all, it's his prize too."

Travis smiled and slipped the knife into his pocket.

After a couple of weeks of looking very ashamed and keeping to himself, Woodrow tried to turn things around by making a joke of it and laughing it off. For a long time, nobody laughed with him, not even my brother Lamar. It got so bad that we even started feeling kind of sorry for him.

One day at school Travis and I sat eating our lunches. Across the school-yard, Woodrow sat on the stone wall, eating all by himself.

"He looks kind of . . . lonely," said Travis.

"Of course he does," I said. "He deserves to."

"You know, I'm not really mad at him anymore. I mean, I was really mad at him for a while. But I'm not really, not anymore." He paused. "Do you think I should tell him?"

I sighed. "I guess so. He looks pretty miserable. And no one else is going to forgive him until you do."

Then Travis did something I'm really proud of. He picked up his lunch bucket and walked across the yard. Woodrow seemed to shrink smaller and smaller as he got closer. All eyes were upon them. We couldn't hear what they said, but Travis stuck out his hand. A second later, Woodrow jumped to his feet and stuck out his hand as well. They shook.

After that, the other kids slowly started talking to him again, and he perked up considerably.

Thus ended the War of the Squirrels. Didn't I warn you it was an

underhanded and unsavory story? I believe I did.

By then, Thud was all grown up. He was almost the size of a bobcat. Viola moved him out to the shack where she lived and got him his own basket. A really big basket. He turned out to be an excellent mouser, just like his mother.

Fluffy, of course, did not turn out to be a mouser. But you could set him loose at the base of a pecan tree and he'd dig you up a nut in three seconds flat.

Don't miss any adventures in the

CALPURNIA TATE
GIRL VET

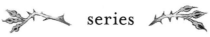

series